BABAR
Loses His Crown

Laurent de Brunhoff

Harry N. Abrams, Inc., Publishers

King Babar and Queen Celeste have been invited
to a special performance at the opera in Paris. Pom,
Flora, and Alexander are coming to Paris, too. So is
Cousin Arthur and his friend Zephir, the monkey.

Celeste and Babar pack their bags for the trip. Babar puts his crown in a little red bag.

The Babar family travels by train.

"I have been to Paris before," says Babar. "I will show you everything."

They get off the train with all their bags. They wait for a taxi.

The taxi takes them to their hotel.

Babar tells the porter, "Be careful with that little red bag. My crown is in it."

In their hotel room, they open all the bags. Celeste
opens the little red one.

"Look!" she cries. "What is this? A flute? Babar! This is
not your bag!"

"My crown! It's lost!" cries Babar. "My crown is gone!"

"I think I know what happened," says Zephir. "When we were waiting for the taxi, I saw a man beside us—a man with a mustache. He must have taken your bag, and you must have taken his."

"I need my crown!" says Babar. "I must wear it to the opera tonight!"

"Don't worry," says Celeste. "We'll find the mustache man. We'll look all over Paris until we do."

So out they go, looking for the man with Babar's bag.

"He may be up in the Eiffel Tower," says Celeste. "All visitors to Paris go there."

They go up to the top of the Eiffel Tower. But they do not see the man with Babar's bag.

"Look at the boats down there!" Arthur shouts. "Let's go for a ride!"

Babar is sad, but he agrees to a boat ride. A boat is ready to take off.

"Captain, wait for us!" shout the children. They climb aboard.

The boat moves toward a bridge. Suddenly Zephir shouts, "Babar, look! Up on the bridge! The mustache man! He is there with your bag!"

The children all shout, "Captain, stop! Stop the boat! Let us off!"

The boat does not stop, so Arthur dives off.
"I'll catch him," he cries. "I'll catch that mustache man!"
Arthur swims to the bank as fast as he can and climbs out
of the water. He is all wet. He sees the man with the bag.

Arthur runs after him. He waves. He yells, "Come back, Mister! You have King Babar's crown!"

But the man has boarded a bus. The bus goes down the street. The mustache man is gone.

In the park, Arthur stands in the sun to dry his clothes.

Suddenly he sees the whole family. They come running toward him.

"I'm glad to see you," he says. "But the red bag—it got away!"

"There's another red bag!" shouts Alexander. He points to a man sitting on a chair. The man is giving crumbs to the birds. "Papa, that bag looks just like yours!"

"Yes, it may be my crown bag," Babar says. "But we must be sure he is the man with the mustache."

They watch the man for a long time.

"I'm sure he's the mustache man," says Zephir.

The Babar family circles around him.
Babar says, "Ahem!"
The man looks up.
He is not the mustache man at all!
"Oh, excuse us," says Babar. "We thought you were someone else."

At lunchtime, Babar takes the family to a sidewalk restaurant.

But Babar is not hungry. He keeps thinking about his crown. He needs to wear it to the opera tonight. But how can he? He fears his crown is lost forever.

Then Arthur jumps up from the table.

"There he is!" yells Arthur. "The man with your crown!"

A man gets into a red taxi. He has a little red bag in his hand.

"Quick!" shouts Babar. "We'll chase him!"

The Babar family climbs into two taxis.

"Follow that red one!" they all shout. A policeman whistles, but they race right past him.

A red light! They have to stop. They are stuck.
The red taxi is gone. Poor Babar! His crown is lost again.

The family gets out of the taxis in front of a market.
Then they see another man with a small red bag!
All the children rush after him. Arthur knocks over
a box of apples. Zephir knocks over a box of fish.

Soon the whole Babar family is chasing the man with the bag.

He runs down the stairs of the subway. They follow him, shouting, "Stop, please, Mr. Mustache!"

Too late! Stuck again! The gates at the bottom of the stairs snap shut.

"Bring back my crown!" shouts Babar.

But the man gets on a train, and the train leaves the station.

Slowly they come up from the subway. Babar says
nothing. He is very, very sad. The children are very tired.
Celeste says to Babar, "We should put the children to
bed in the hotel. Then we will go to the opera."

Back in the hotel room, Celeste and Babar say good night to the children. The three littlest ones are already half asleep.

Celeste has put on her best dress. She offers to let Babar wear her crown for the evening.

"Thank you, that is so kind of you," he says, "but it is too small. I will go with no crown at all."

They arrive at the big opera house. They see hundreds of people going inside.

"Oh, dear," sighs Babar. "All those people will see me, the King of the Elephants, without a crown! I just can't go in there!"

Then, *BANG!*

A man bumps into
Babar. A man with a
bag! The mustache man!

They open their bags, and Babar says, "My crown! I can wear a crown. But I can't wear a flute."

The mustache man smiles and says, "My flute! I can play a flute. But I can't play a crown."

It turns out to be a great night after all. The crown is on the head of the king . . .

. . . and the flute is under the mustache man's mustache.

Production Manager: Jonathan Lopes

Library of Congress Cataloging-in-Publication Data

Brunhoff, Laurent de, 1925–
Babar loses his crown / by Laurent de Brunhoff.
p. cm.
Summary: Babar and his family see the sights of Paris while trying to find the man
who accidentally switched his bag with the one containing Babar's crown.
ISBN 0-8109-5034-0
[1. Lost and found possessions—Fiction. 2. Elephants—Fiction. 3. Kings, queens, rulers, etc.—Fiction.
4. Paris (France)—Fiction. 5. France—Fiction.] I. Title.

PZ7.B828443Baan 2004
[E]—dc22
2003024710

Printed and bound in Mexico
10 9 8 7 6 5 4 3 2 1

Harry N. Abrams, Inc. 100 Fifth Avenue, New York, NY 10011
www.abramsbooks.com

Abrams is a subsidiary of
LA MARTINIÈRE